The Bears BITE BACK

by

Derek Keilty

Illustrated by Vince Reid

First published
January 08 in Great Britain by

PUBLISHING

Educational Printing Services Limited
Albion Mill, Water Street, Great Harwood, Blackburn BB6 7QR
Telephone: (01254) 882080   Fax: (01254) 882010
E-mail: enquiries@eprint.co.uk   Website: www.eprint.co.uk

Contents

'For my wife, Elaine,
With Love'

The Bears  BACK

Chapter 1

Bears

'The cheek of her,' said Mummy Bear.

'Breaking an' entering, that's what it is!' growled Daddy Bear.

'And my favourite chair will never be the same,' sobbed Baby Bear.

All was not well in the Bears' house.

Their intruder, Goldilocks, had left the place in a right old state.

Daddy Bear dipped the broken leg of Baby Bear's chair in some honey and shoved it back into the wooden seat. But when he set it up, the chair fell apart again.

Baby Bear burst into tears. 'It's ruined!'

Mummy Bear was mad. 'Phone Sergeant Plonk to see if he's caught the culprit yet,' she told Daddy Bear.

But Daddy Bear shook his head. 'I phoned ten minutes ago. He says he's still making enquiries.'

Mummy Bear clenched her fists. 'Who does she think she is prancing in here like she owns the place? I wish I could go over to her house and give her a piece of my mind.'

'That's it!' Daddy Bear shrieked. 'But we'll do better than that. We'll go and eat her porridge, break her furniture and sleep in her bed!'

'Yeah, and see how she likes it,' cried Baby Bear.

'Good idea. I'm starving. I had to throw

all our porridge out after she'd stuck her grubby little paws in it,' said Mummy Bear.

'Yuk! Girl germs!' said Baby Bear.

'Right that's settled then - let's go.'

'Hang on,' said Mummy Bear. 'Go where? We don't even know where she lives.'

'We're bears aren't we?' Daddy Bear grinned. 'We'll follow her paw prints.'

'Feet,' Baby Bear corrected, 'humans have feet.'

'Whatever,' sighed Daddy Bear.

And with that, the three bears locked up their house and set off following the trail of footprints...

Chapter 2
Goldi

Goldilocks stuck her head out of her bedroom window and gasped. Sergeant Plonk was at the door, asking for her. In a panic, she pulled off her porridge-stained T-shirt and shoved it under her bed. But as she did, she spotted a big bruise on her elbow. She'd got it this morning when she'd fallen off Baby Bear's chair. She flew round her bedroom, flinging clothes out of drawers, until she found her long sleeve T-shirt. 'Perfect,' she sighed.

Mum was shouting up at her. 'Goldi, come down at once!'

Quickly tucking a golden lock of hair into her baseball cap, Goldilocks skipped downstairs. 'Oh hello, Sergeant Plonk.'

'Were you anywhere near the Bears' house, today?' Mum asked.

'Not me,' she replied, 'I've been tidying my room all morning.' Double fib. Not only had she been at the Bears' house, her room looked like a bomb had hit it!

Sergeant Plonk peered at his notebook. 'An intruder broke into the Bears' house. They said it was a little girl with blonde ringlets.'

This made Goldilocks' mum a bit cross.
'There are loads of little blonde girls in
town. It could have been any of them.'

Goldilocks felt a goldy lock of hair
spring out from under her cap. Her face
went whiter than a snowman's ghost.
Sergeant Plonk's beady eyes squinted at her
as she quickly shoved it back up.

'Besides, Goldi's afraid of bears,' Mum went on. 'She never goes anywhere near the woods. Do you?'

'Er, no Mum,' Goldilocks stuttered. 'Maybe the intruder was wearing a disguise?' asked Goldilocks.

'A curly blonde wig, hmm, I doubt it,' Sergeant Plonk sighed. 'Right then, I'll be off then. If you hear anything let me know.'

Mum scratched her head. 'Who on earth would break into the Bears' house?'

Goldilocks shrugged. 'Dunno.'

'Goldi, are you all right? You've gone a funny colour.'

'I'm just a bit tired; I think I'll go up to my room.'

Goldilocks went up to her room and slumped on her bed. She felt awful...like a criminal. She didn't mean to break the little chair and the porridge really had smelt delicious. She decided to lie low for a while. She'd stay indoors for a few days. She marked the little teddy bear calendar above her bed.

Goldilocks hoped that by then, Sergeant Plonk and the bears would have forgotten all about it.

But at that moment, the bears were tramping through the forest, hungry for revenge - not to mention porridge!

Chapter 3

Revenge

The three bears were quite the experts at following footprints and soon they were outside Goldilocks' front door.

'So this is where the little rascal lives!' growled Daddy Bear. And with his big bear foot, he broke down the door.

Goldilocks was watching TV and her

mum was finishing the supper when the
bears burst in. First Daddy Bear, then
Mummy Bear and last of all Baby Bear.
Goldilocks screamed and dived behind the
sofa.

Her mum shrieked dropping a plate,
which shattered on the floor.

'Careful, you'll ruin supper,' called Mummy Bear.

'Get out of my house!' yelled Goldilocks' mum.

Daddy Bear pretended to look hurt. 'That's not a very nice way to greet your dinner guests.'

'Get out or I'll call Sergeant Plonk.' Mummy Bear handed her the phone. 'Go ahead. It's about time you told him it was your daughter who broke into our house.'

Goldilocks' mum gasped. 'Don't be so silly. My daughter's been home all day.' Goldilocks shrank further behind the sofa. She wished the floor would open up and swallow her.

'We followed her footprints,' said

Mummy Bear, 'they led us to your house.'

'Goldi, tell me this isn't true?'

Goldilocks burst out crying. 'I didn't mean to break the little chair and the porridge smelt sooo good.'

'So you did break into the Bears' house?'

'I didn't break in. They left the door open, I just... I'm sorry.'

'Wicked rascals like her need to be taught a lesson!' boomed Daddy Bear.

'Yeah, now it's our turn,' said Baby Bear.

'What do you want?' asked Mum trembling.

Daddy bear strode towards Mum, drooling from the corners of his mouth.

'Something to eat...'

'Ahh! You can't eat me,' Mum shrieked. 'I'd...I'd taste horrible!'

Chapter 4
Sleepy Heads

'Smells like pizza,' said Daddy Bear shoving Mum out of the way as he rushed to the kitchen.

'S'pose it'll do,' said Mummy Bear snatching the pizza out of the oven and slicing it up.

'But that's our supper,' moaned Mum.

'Too bad - Goldilocks ruined our supper,' snapped Baby Bear.

Daddy Bear tasted it first. 'Pha!' he spat it out. 'Too much pepperoni.'

Mummy Bear tried some. 'Yuk! Too much mushroom.'

Baby Bear munched a bit. 'Mmm. I think it's just right.'

Mummy Bear stomped about the kitchen, pulling cartons from cupboards and food from the fridge. Finally she found a big box of porridge oats. She shoved the box into Mum's hand. 'You're going to make us two extra large bowls of porridge.'

Daddy Bear went to sit down in the armchair. 'Yeah, we'll have it in front of the telly.'

Goldilocks cringed. She was sure the chair was far too small for him. There was a loud splitting sound as one arm of the armchair snapped completely off. Mummy Bear did the same to the other armchair.

'My good furniture,' howled Mum.

'Goldilocks broke my favourite chair,' grumbled Baby Bear. He plonked right in the middle of the sofa and munched his pizza.

Daddy Bear scratched his head. 'I've got an idea.' He broke off both arms from either end of the sofa and shoved the two armless armchairs at either end, making a very long super sofa. Then, he sat at one end while Mummy Bear sat at the other end with Baby Bear in the middle.

'That's more like it,' he beamed.

Goldilocks' mum carried two steaming bowls of porridge from the kitchen and gave them to the bears.

'About time too,' they growled ungratefully.

The three bears ate their supper watching one of Goldilocks' favourite DVD's, Winnie the Pooh. When they'd finished Daddy Bear yawned. 'I'm sleepy.'

'Me too,' said Mummy Bear.

'Me three,' said Baby Bear. 'I could sleep for a week.'

'No point rushing home when we can sleep here,' said Daddy Bear.

Goldilocks' mum flung her hands in the air. 'You can't sleep here!'

'Try an' stop us,' shouted Daddy Bear as the three bears stomped upstairs. Daddy Bear flopped on Mum's double bed. Mummy Bear lay on the bed in the spare room. Baby Bear crawled into Goldilocks' bed. And they all fell fast asleep.

Goldilocks' mum was in a foul mood. 'This is all your fault, Goldi,' she said. 'Why didn't you tell me?'

'I was frightened,' explained Goldilocks.

'Maybe they'll go in the morning,' she went on, trying to sound hopeful.

That night, Goldilocks and her mum had to sleep on the super sofa.

But the bears didn't leave in the morning. They didn't even wake up. They slept all day and all night for three whole

days. Goldilocks marked her calendar with an 'X' as each day went by.

Finally, Goldilocks' mum announced, 'That's it, I'm calling Sergeant Plonk.'

Goldilocks felt a lump in her throat. Now she was for it.

Sergeant Plonk soon arrived in a flap. 'I wish you'd told me in the first place,' he huffed. Then he gave Goldilocks a lecture on not telling lies.

He tried to wake the bears but couldn't. Goldilocks sat miserably on her bed staring at her calendar. Then suddenly an awful thought sprang into her head.

'Hang on, I think I know why the bears won't wake up!' she gasped. 'It's December.'

Sergeant Plonk stared at her.
'December, so what?'

'What are you talking about?' said Mum.

'Don't you see? It's wintertime,' she
cried. 'Bears hibernate in the winter!'

Chapter 5
The Plan

'Hibernating!' shrieked Mum. 'But that means they'll be asleep on our beds till spring.'

'If that's the case then there really isn't anything I can do,' sighed Sergeant Plonk. 'If I try to shift them I'll have animal welfare breathing down my neck!' He turned to leave.

'But they can't stay here all winter.'

'Well maybe you should've thought of that before you went breaking into their house.'

'I didn't break in, the door... oh never mind.'

When Sergeant Plonk left, Mum sank to her knees. 'What on earth are we going to do?'

'Well it's obvious they're not going to wake up themselves,' said Goldilocks, thinking aloud. 'So that means we've got to wake them up.'

'Wake them up, but how?'

Goldilocks picked up the phone. 'I've got an idea.'

'Who are you phoning?' Mum asked.

Goldilocks smiled. 'Hello, eh yes, I wondered if you played anything louder than a flute. You do - great! Can you come over? Oh and hurry... it's a bit of an emergency.'

In half an hour, a skinny man, wearing a red and yellow, striped tunic, arrived. He took off his hat, which had a feather sticking out of it and bowed an extremely low bow. 'The Pied Piper at your service.'

Goldilocks took him upstairs. 'I need you to wake up three very sleepy bears.'

'A bit bigger than rats but I'll have a go,' he chuckled.

Taking out his flute, he played it as loud as he could. He played it right beside their ears. He hit some very high notes. The glass

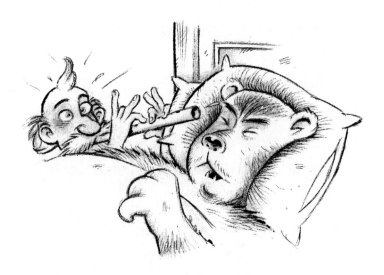

on one of Goldilocks' pictures shattered. As he played he marched in and out of the three bedrooms. Goldilocks couldn't help herself following him. And with mum following too, they made a sort of a train.

But the bears didn't wake up.

'Not to worry,' said the Pied Piper, 'I've brought some back up.'

Opening a big black case, he took out

the most enormous set of bagpipes. 'This should do the trick.'

Cheeks puffed out like two rosy apples, the Pied Piper blasted a tune on the bagpipes. The din was so awful, Goldilocks held her ears. But still the bears slept soundly. Daddy Bear began to snore almost as loudly as the bagpipes.

Mum fumed. 'It's hopeless.'

'Can't you do anything to wake them?' asked Goldilocks desperately.

'I can't.' The Pied Piper stroked his pointy chin and thought hard. 'But don't panic, I think I know someone who can.'

Chapter 6

Prince Charming

'He's been gone for ages,' sighed Goldilocks.

'Probably forgotten about us,' said Goldilocks' mum gloomily. 'Now we're stuck with three bears all winter.'

They were waiting for the Pied Piper. He told them he'd come back with help but hadn't told them what he was planning.

Suddenly, they heard horses' hooves outside. Goldilocks stared out of the window in disbelief. A beautiful golden carriage pulled up outside. Prince Charming got out, royal robes flowing behind him.

'I hope this won't take long, Piper,' groaned the Prince. 'I'm late for a ball.'

'Just a few of your magic kisses, your Royal Highness,' said the Pied Piper.

Goldilocks and Mum both grinned with delight. They curtsied to the Prince then brought him inside.

Striding into Goldilocks' bedroom, Prince Charming saw Baby Bear asleep on Goldilocks' bed. 'Bears!' he yelled. 'You never told me they were bears.'

'Oh please Your Highness,' pleaded Goldilocks, 'you're our only hope,'

'I've never kissed a bear in my life. Yuk!'

'Oh go on, just a quick peck on the cheek,' coaxed the Pied Piper.

'Otherwise we'll be stuck with them all winter,' cried Mum.

The Prince broke out in a sweat. 'Oh very well then. But one kiss each. If it doesn't work I'm leaving.'

'Deal!' said Goldilocks.

The Prince took out a huge silk handkerchief and leaned over Baby Bear, kissing him gently on the forehead.

Goldilocks held her breath. Baby Bear didn't move. The Prince shrugged. 'Maybe it doesn't work on bears, only princesses.'

'Probably takes time to work,' suggested Goldilocks. 'C'mon you might as well kiss the other bears too.'

She took him into Mum's room next.

Sprawled out like a mountain was Daddy Bear.

The Prince wiped his mouth with his handkerchief. Closing his eyes, he leaned over and gave Daddy Bear a pretend kiss on the forehead.

'That's no good,' cried Goldilocks, 'it's got to be a real kiss.'

The Prince sighed. 'Oh very well then.'

He puckered up again and gave Daddy Bear the smallest of pecks on the forehead.

'Yuk!' he choked, wiping his mouth.

Daddy Bear made a loud grunting noise and turned over.

'One more,' cried Goldilocks.

In the spare room, the Prince gave Mummy Bear a kiss. They all stood watching, but for the third time nothing happened. Goldilocks' face was glum. Then suddenly Mummy Bear opened an eye. She stared dreamily at the prince. 'Your Royal Highness.'

'Sorry to wake you, but I'm afraid you're hibernating in this poor family's house.'

But Mummy Bear wasn't listening she'd gone all gooey. She flung her arms round the Prince's neck.

'Does this always happen?' Goldilocks' mum asked.

'Perils of the job, I'm afraid,' choked the Prince trying to wriggle free.

Then a voice boomed. 'What are you doing hugging my wife?' It was Daddy Bear - awake and by the look on his face, very, very angry!

Chapter 7

A Big Surprise

'As I was just explaining...'

'Get away from her before I thump you,' growled Daddy Bear.

'You can't thump the Prince,' the Prince protested.

But Daddy Bear grabbed him by the

collar and lifted him right up to the ceiling.
'Put me down you big oaf or I'll tell the King.'

'Leave him alone,' shouted Goldilocks.

Daddy Bear reached out his other huge
hand and grabbed Goldilocks. 'This is
probably your doing. You're nothing but
trouble.' He pulled her up to his snarling
face. Goldilocks could see right inside his
mouth. He had some ferocious looking teeth

in there and his breath smelt of old socks. She closed her eyes...

Then, suddenly she heard someone shriek. It came from her room. It sounded like Baby Bear.

Daddy Bear dropped his captives and they all rushed into Goldilocks' bedroom. Baby Bear was standing on the bed staring at Goldilocks' little calendar.

'What's the matter, son?' Mummy Bear asked.

'I... I don't believe it. Is it really the fifth of December?' he asked, pointing at the calendar.

'Er... yes,' said Goldilocks.

Baby Bear did a back flip on the bed.

'It's today. It's today!' he whooped.

'What's today?' Daddy Bear frowned.

'My birthday - isn't it Mum?'

Mummy Bear thought for a moment then nodded. 'Er... yes.'

'I can't believe it. Every year we miss it 'cause we're hibernating.'

'Hang on,' said Goldilocks, 'are you saying you've never had a birthday party?'

Baby Bear shook his head. 'Seven birthdays and I've slept through every last one of them - till now!'

The Pied Piper gasped.

The Prince shook his head. 'That's

dreadful.'

'Hard to believe,' said Goldilocks' mum.

Baby Bear looked up at his dad with big bear eyes then asked. 'Dad, can I have a birthday party?'

'Of course you can, son... er what's a birthday party?'

Goldilocks smiled, 'We could help.'

'Provided you go home afterwards,' Goldilocks' mum added quickly.

'Oh please Mum, can we?' Baby Bear pleaded.

And for the first time, Mummy Bear actually smiled. 'That's... kind of you,' she said.

Daddy Bear smiled too. 'Er we won't press charges. And we promise to tidy up and leave you alone.'

Goldilocks smiled, 'That's settled then.'

'Hang on,' said the Prince, 'if he hasn't had a birthday in all his seven years then it can't be just any old birthday party - it's got to be the best birthday party ever!'

Chapter 8

The Party

Baby Bear's first ever birthday party went with a huge bang.

The Prince forgot all about the ball. Instead he took Goldilocks and Baby Bear to the palace to pick a birthday cake from the palace kitchen. Not forgetting the seven candles.

While they were gone, Daddy Bear fixed the sofa and armchairs and decorated the room with streamers and balloons.

Mummy Bear helped Goldilocks' mum tidy the kitchen and make the party food. Mummy Bear even gave Goldilocks' mum her secret recipe for carrot and chocolate porridge.

During the party, the Pied Piper played 'Happy Birthday' on the flute and everyone sang along. After he'd finished he presented the flute to Baby Bear. 'This is for you, happy birthday.'

'Wow, thanks a lot,' gasped Baby Bear.

'I've something for you too,' said Goldilocks taking out a brown parcel. She'd made a secret stop on the way back from the palace.

Baby Bear tore the wrapping off the oddly shaped present then shrieked. 'A new chair! It's mega, thank you.' He tried it out and it was just right.

From that day on, Goldilocks had a new friend and was far too busy playing to go breaking into houses.

And yes, this time they all really did live happily ever after... they really did y'know!

Cillyderella

Chapter 1
Scrambled Eggs

Cillyderella was very, very silly.

She wore multi-coloured dungarees, stripy tights, and fluffy bunny slippers. Her hair was a different colour and different silly style every day of the week.

Not only did she look silly, she acted

silly. She'd break dance around the castle she lived in with her stepmother and two stepsisters, to her favourite silly songs by Aggy and the Pipsqueaks, (she called it break dancing because usually she'd end up crashing into something and breaking it).

'You'll be right through that ceiling one day - then you'll be in for it!' her stepsisters would yell at her.

And she loved telling jokes. She knew hundreds and kept them all in a special joke book. She told them to everyone - even her pet frog.

Although Cillyderella was silly, she was very kind. Not like her stepmother and stepsisters who were mean - especially to Cillyderella. They made Cillyderella do all the chores around the house. They made her scrub the floors, make the dinner and wash their clothes. And if she complained her stepmother would threaten to take away her joke book and silly CD's.

'Cillyderella, have you got breakfast ready yet, I'm starving?' grumbled Griselda one morning. Griselda was a plump girl with black hair in a big bun. She was always hungry.

Felicity wiped her knife with a napkin. She was skinny with blonde hair and a terrible fusspot. 'What's keeping you?' she shouted.

Cillyderella hurried out of the kitchen with a big plate of scrambled egg.

'What's a frog's favourite drink?' asked Cillyderella.

Griselda sighed. 'I don't know. What is a frog's favourite drink?'

'Croaka-cola!' Cillyderella shrieked, almost dropping the plate.

'Careful with my scrambled eggs you idiot!' growled Griselda. 'I don't want them any more scrambled than they already are.'

Griselda grabbed the brown sauce and squeezed almost the whole bottle over her scrambled eggs.

'You're disgusting, Griselda,' said Felicity.

'And you're stuck up!'

'Am not!'

'Are too!' Griselda put out her tongue then slurped her scrambled egg.

'Phaaa! This is cold!' she spat.

Cillyderella gasped. 'But I've just made

it. You've probably put too much sauce on it.'

'Make some fresh stuff!' Griselda boomed at her.

Griselda had just lifted her plate to give to Cillyderella when suddenly...

'BOO!' screamed a voice behind her.

Griselda jumped, tossing her plate up in the air. The scrambled egg splatted all over her head.

She turned round but there was no one there. 'Look at this mess. That was your fault, Cillyderella,' she shouted.

'But it wasn't me, honest,' said Cillyderella trying not to laugh.

Just then, Lady Muggly appeared. With her black hair, pointy nose and thin staring eyes, she was almost witch-like.

'What on earth's going on?' she demanded.

'It's Cillyderella's fault,' cried Griselda.

'She's being silly again,' said Felicity.

Her stepmother scowled at her. 'Clean

this mess up at once, you horrid little worm, before I throttle you! Then go to your room.'

Cillyderella did as she was told.

Later in her room, she sat by her poster of the prince and talked to her pet frog, 'I don't know who scared Griselda but it wasn't me.'

'Ribbet ribbet!' croaked the frog, hopping onto her head.

She giggled. 'Mind you she did look ridiculous with that scrambled egg on her head.'

'BOO!' said a voice behind her; the same voice that had frightened Griselda.

'What on earth...?' Cillyderella looked round to see a small fairy dressed all in black with a pale, kind face, sitting on her window ledge. The fairy chuckled.

'Gotcha!'

Cillyderella stared. She'd read books about fairies, but she'd never seen a real one.

'Who are you?'

The fairy smiled. 'I'm your Scary Godmother and we are going to be the silliest and bestest of friends...'

Chapter 2
Mirror! Mirror!

'If you smiled your face would crack!' said the King, that afternoon at the Royal palace.

'What's there to smile about?' moaned the Prince, rocking his throne on two legs.

The Queen burst into the room,

struggling with a huge parcel. 'You'll never guess what I've bought?' She pulled off the wrapper.

'A rusty old mirror!' said the King.

'A magic mirror,' corrected the Queen. 'I got it at Snow White's carriage boot sale. It can answer questions, and tell you how gorgeous you look.'

She noticed the Prince's long face. 'What's wrong with him?' she asked the King.

'The usual - he's fed up!'

'All my good looks and you're fed up,' tutted the Queen, fixing her hair in front of the mirror. 'What you need is to meet a nice princess.'

'A princess!' Gasping, the Prince fell backwards off his throne. He got up rubbing his head. 'A princess would make me more miserable - girls are so boring.'

'We could hold a ball I s'pose,' said the King who liked the Queen's idea.

'A grand ball and invite all the ladies of the Kingdom. They can't all be boring.' said the Queen.

The Prince sighed. 'Oh Mother must we? I hate all that awful dancing and trying to think of what to say.'

'Why don't we ask the magic mirror what it thinks? If it really is magic,' said the King.

'Great idea,' said the Queen.

'Mirror, Mirror on the wall, should we

hold a palace ball?' she asked the mirror.

The mirror misted over then a spooky voice said.

The answers yes and do not tarry,
If you want the Prince to marry.

The Queen smiled a beaming smile. 'Great! That's settled then. I'll send out the invitations.'

Chapter 3
A Royal Invitation

'What a stroke of luck!' cried Lady
Muggly hurrying along the hall the next
morning. She was holding a gold letter.

'What's that?' chorused Felicity and
Griselda rushing out to meet her.

Cillyderella stopped scrubbing the

stairs and looked horrified. 'Careful I've just washed...'

Too late. Lady Muggly slipped on the wet floor, did a sort of break dance (the kind Cillyderella practised in her room), and fell flat on her bottom.

Lady Muggly scowled at Cillyderella. Griselda snatched the letter out of her hand. She read:

The King and Queen cordially invite you and your

daughters to a Grand Ball at the

Royal palace tonight.

Formal dress please.

'Awesome!' cried Griselda. 'Now's my chance to get the Prince to marry me. Then

I'll be rich and get to eat scrummy palace food every day.' She stuffed a whole slice of toast in her mouth.

Felicity grabbed the letter. 'Dream on, he's more likely to fall in love with me. I'd make a beautiful princess. And with my manners I'd fit in perfectly at the palace.' She curtsied, fanning out her dress.

'I've got manners too!' growled Griselda.

'Yeah - of a PIG!'

'Will you both be quiet,' shouted Lady Muggly snatching back the letter. 'Don't you see, this is our big chance. But there's no time for bickering, we have to start getting ready.'

Cillyderella took Griselda's hands. 'Maybe the Prince will fall in love with me. Mind you, ballroom dancing is soooo boring. They should call it boring room dancing.' She waltzed down the hallway then, letting go of Griselda's hands, she did the splits and spun on her back. 'But that's okay; I'll teach everyone how to break dance!'

Lady Muggly looked at her with disgust. 'You're not coming, Cillyderella!'

Cillyderella stopped spinning and got to her knees. 'What?'

'You heard me. Only the three of us are invited.'

'But it doesn't say I'm not invited,' said Cillyderella.

"Course you're not invited. You're too silly,' snapped Griselda.

'Anyway you don't have a posh dress, all your clothes look ridiculous,' added Felicity.

Cillyderella's heart sank. She ran into

her room to have a good cry when...

'Boo!' It was her Scary Godmother, hiding behind her bedroom door.

'I wish you wouldn't keep doing that!' sobbed Cillyderella.

'What on earth's the matter?' asked the fairy, noticing how upset Cillyderella was.

'They won't let me go to the ball.'

'What ball?'

'At the palace.' She pointed at her poster. 'With the Prince.'

'Why can't you go?'

'They say I'm too silly and don't have a dress.'

The Scary Godmother looked cross. 'The rotters! Well you're not too silly and you will have a dress, the prettiest dress in the whole kingdom!'

Cillyderella stopped sobbing and frowned at her. 'What are you saying?'

'I'm saying you ARE going to the ball. Just leave everything to me.'

Chapter 4
Fairy Magic

On the night of the ball, Cillyderella waved goodbye to her stepmother and stepsisters at the front door.

'Make sure you tidy all my dresses up,' called Felicity having a final check in the mirror.

Griselda drained a bottle of coke and tossed the bottle to Cillyderella. 'Burp! And have some pizza ready for us when we come back.'

Her stepmother sneered, 'and no stupid pranks while we're out!'

Cillyderella nodded, trying to hide her excitement at her Scary Godmother's promise.

And as soon as they left, she appeared. 'Boo! Time we got busy.'

They went out to the back of the castle. Handing an old potato sack to Cillyderella, the fairy opened her spell book.

'Now, pop your head through that sack.'

Cillyderella looked puzzled but did as she was told. The Scary Godmother waved her magic wand and in a flash the sack turned into a fancy pink ball gown.

'Wow!' cried Cillyderella.

'Do you like it?'

'It's great, though I'm not sure I could do much break dancing in it.'

'Now what else...'

'My hair - how about pink to go with the dress?' suggested Cillyderella.

"Fraid not - you've got to conform deary.'

'Con- what?'

'Fit in!'

Lifting a bird's nest, she placed it on Cillyderella's head then waved her magic wand.

In a puff of smoke her hair was up in a beautiful bun with netting and glitter.

'I think you're ready,' exclaimed the Scary Godmother. 'Now all we have to do is get you there - in style.'

Opening the shed, she wheeled out Griselda's old orange bike with buckled wheels. 'This should do the trick.'

Magically, the bike transformed into a pumpkin coloured stretch limousine with black windows.

'Awesome,' cried Cillyderella, 'can I get in?'

'Be my guest.'

Inside, Cillyderella gasped. There was a television and DVD player not to mention a fridge full of lemonade and her favourite chocolates. 'Maybe I'll stay in here all night,' she joked. Then she looked a bit glum. 'Oh but I can't drive. How am I...'

As she spoke, the Scary Godmother waved the wand over her own head. In a flash her clothes changed into a black suit with a shirt and tie and a peak cap. And some cool, mirror lens sunglasses.

'Your chauffairy godmother - at your service ma'am!' she saluted, grinning.

Cillyderella giggled and moments later they set off out of the castle gates.

Chapter 5
Ballroom Blitz

The fairy was quite a demon driver and they arrived at the palace in record time.

'Oh I almost forgot - the spell wears off at midnight, so you'll need to be home before then. Have fun!' she told Cillyderella, as she let her out of the limo.

Cillyderella nodded, waving goodbye.
'Thanks sooo much, you're the coolest Fairy
Godmother in the universe.'

Inside the ballroom, couples were
already dancing to a slow waltz. Cillyderella
wondered why anyone would want to dance
to such dreary music.

The Prince wasn't dancing. He was
standing near the King and Queen.
Cillyderella thought he looked bored.

Cillyderella noticed Felicity and Griselda
scuttling sideways like two crabs to get
closer to the Prince. Their mother was
elbowing them to keep moving.

But the Prince wasn't asking anyone to

dance.

'I wouldn't dance with him even if he paid me!' said a skinny girl standing next to Cillyderella.

'Why not?' asked Cillyderella.

'He's a bit of a bore.'

Cillyderella giggled. 'Well, that music's awful. And the dancing - no wonder he's bored!'

Later on, Cillyderella felt a tap on her shoulder. She turned round and to her surprise saw it was the Queen.

'Y...your majesty,' she stuttered,

starting to curtsy.

The Queen smiled then whispered in her ear. 'I think you're quite the prettiest girl here. Would you please do me a service and dance with my son before I murder him?'

Cillyderella was flabbergasted. She glanced at the skinny girl who rolled her eyes then said, 'I...I'd love to.'

So Cillyderella danced with the Prince. Not break dancing though - boring room dancing as she called it.

The Prince didn't speak. Even when the Queen had introduced Cillyderella, he'd just grunted.

Cillyderella began to think her friend had been right. He was a bore. And a rude one too.

The music finished and Cillyderella smiled politely though she was glad it was over. She'd had more fun scrubbing the stairs.

Before she sat down, she curtsied fanning out her dress. The Prince bowed low, then lower, then froze, staring at the floor. Cillyderella looked down to see what he was looking at and gasped. Peeking out of the front of her dress were her fluffy bunny slippers. Her Scary Godmother had forgotten to change them into proper shoes.

The Prince began to chuckle, then laughed louder and louder until tears streamed down his face.

'They are the most amazing slippers!' he gasped.

'They're my favourites!' she grinned, remembering a joke. 'What do you get if you pour boiling water down a rabbit hole?'

The Prince shook his head, 'I don't know.'

'Hot cross bunnies.'

The Prince burst into more fits of laughter then asked, 'Do you know any more?

'Loads!' Cillyderella grinned.

The next thing, the band started playing again.

'Can you break dance?'

'Er no, what's that?'

'It's a cool dance I know. I can teach you if you like?'

'Okay!'

'But first we need some cool vibes. I'll be back in a tick.'

Fetching her CD player from the limo, Cillyderella gave the band a rest and blasted out Ballroom Blitz by Aggy and the Pipsqueaks.

Cillyderella showed the Prince some break

dancing moves and he tried to copy them.

'Not bad,' she praised.

The Queen beamed a huge smile at the King. She was so pleased.

'I was beginning to think he was always going to be miserable,' said the King.

Griselda and Felicity watched horrified.

'That's that horrid dancing Cillyderella does,' said Griselda.

Felicity put her nose in the air. 'The Prince is doing it - how common!'

But Cillyderella was having trouble with some of her moves. 'It's hopeless in this dress and all these pins in my hair are driving me bonkers.'

The Prince nodded, 'I know I hate this stuffy suit too. Why not take your hair out - bathroom's just upstairs,' he suggested.

'Great!' Cillyderella hurried upstairs.

'Wow, this bathroom's bigger than my bedroom,' she gasped looking round for the mirror. She fiddled about taking all the pins out of her hair. But just as she was almost finished she heard the clock strike midnight.

Suddenly, before her very eyes, her hair zapped back into pink, gelled spikes with red ribbons. Her ball gown became her multi-coloured dungarees and stripy tights. It was too good to be true.

'Great timing, now I can show the Prince how I really dress.' She rushed out of the bathroom only to feel a hand grab her.

'Oh no you don't!' It was a big burly palace footman. 'Ladies only that way and I don't think we ordered a clown. How'd you sneak in anyway?'

Cillyderella was frantic. 'B...But I'm a guest!' she cried.

'Ha! Pull the other one. You're leaving right now!'

And he led her down the back staircase and shoved her out of the palace.

'No need to push, you've made me lose one of my slippers!' she yelped.

It was pouring outside and in seconds Cillyderella was totally soaking. She couldn't go back to the Prince now.

At the front of the palace, the limo had turned back into an old rusty bicycle. She pedalled home feeling miserable.

Chapter 6
An Evil Plan

The next day the doorbell at Lady
Muggly's castle rang.

Lady Muggly screamed for Cillyderella
to get it but she was still sulking in her
room, playing sad CD's. She missed the
Prince.

'Insolent child - I'll get it myself then!'

A palace footman stood at the door and behind him - the Prince himself.

'Do come in Your Royal Highness. To what do we owe the honour?' she said curtseying.

'A royal decree ma'am,' declared the footman holding up the fluffy bunny slipper. 'The maid whose foot fits this slipper shall marry the Prince!'

Lady Muggly stared at the slipper. She recognized it was Cillyderella's but suddenly had an evil plan. Bringing her guests into the sitting room, she hurried upstairs and locked Cillyderella's bedroom door from the outside. Then she found Felicity and

Griselda and almost shoved them downstairs.

'The kind footman's returned your slipper,' she winked. 'Now one of you shall marry the Prince.'

In the sitting room, Griselda grabbed the slipper off the footman. 'It's mine!'

But Felicity snatched one end. 'Give it back. It's mine you big oaf!'

'You're stretching it,' cried the footman.

'Sit down both of you,' shouted the Prince taking back the slipper.

The footman tried it on Felicity's foot - it fitted perfectly.

'Told you!' she cried excitedly.

The Prince was stunned. 'Then... it is you shall be my bride!'

The Scary Godmother who'd been watching from the window, gasped. Then quickly disappeared to tell Cillyderella.

Cillyderella was outraged. 'But Lady Muggly knows that's my slipper!'

'Then you must hurry downstairs and prove it's yours,' cried the Scary Godmother. But when Cillyderella tried the door it was locked.

'Someone's locked the door,' gasped Cillyderella. 'Can you open it with a spell?'

The Scary Godmother tried but shook her head. 'Must've been that ol' witch Lady Muggly, she's put a spell on it - I can't budge it!'

Cillyderella turned down her CD to help her think, when suddenly she froze. 'Hang on, I've got an idea!' She turned it up again full blast then she began break dancing round her bedroom.

'Er shouldn't we be thinking of a way out of here?' said the Scary Godmother scratching her head.

Chapter 7
In the End

Lady Muggly shrieked. 'A royal wedding, whatever will I wear?'

Felicity stood at the magic mirror. 'Oh but I must change immediately. A princess must look her best, mustn't she?'

'Tell us one of your jokes,' the Prince asked suspiciously.

Felicity was taken aback. 'Jokes?'

'Yes, you told me you knew hundreds.'

'Eh - I do. What's a frog's favourite drink?' she stuttered, trying to think of one of Cillyderella's.

'I don't know. What is a frog's favourite drink?'

But she couldn't remember the punch line. Finally she blurted out, 'Milk.'

'That joke wasn't even funny,' barked Griselda.

Felicity kicked her. But as she did, the slipper flew off. And the handkerchief she'd stuffed inside it to keep it on her foot fell out. Her cheeks went as red as a raspberry.

'Rotten cheat! Told you it was mine. Give it here!' Griselda screeched.

The Prince's patience was wearing thin. He picked up the slipper. 'You don't look a bit like the girl I danced with. And I'm fairly sure you don't know how to break dance.'

'Course I do,' said Griselda. And next thing she was charging across the room, sliding onto her knees. She crashed through the kitchen doors and rolled, spinning onto her back and bumping her head on the kitchen table.

They all rushed in after her. 'Are you all

right, madam?' asked the footman.

'Think so,' she groaned.

The Prince rolled his eyes. 'This is a waste of time.' Then suddenly he heard music and thumping noises above his head.

'What on earth is that noise? Have you got a herd of elephants upstairs?' he asked frowning.

Lady Muggly gasped, realising Cillyderella's room was right above the kitchen. She quickly thought of an excuse, 'Must be the servants cleaning behind the furniture.'

'Do you have any more daughters?' the

footman cut in.

Lady Muggly shook her head.

A crack appeared in the ceiling. Some dust sprinkled onto Lady Muggly's nose.

'Are you sure,' probed the footman. He opened a scroll. 'It says here that you have three daughters.'

More cracks appeared in the ceiling. Lady Muggly fumed. 'Then it's wrong!'

'Y'know that music sounds very familiar,' said the Prince.

CRASH! With a loud bang and a thick cloud of dust, a leg suddenly came right through the kitchen ceiling - Cillyderella's leg complete with multi coloured stripy tights.

She wiggled her toes.

'It's my slipper! It's my slipper!' came a faint voice through the ceiling.

The Prince glowered at Lady Muggly. 'I demand to know what's going on? Who is this girl?'

'It's Cillyderella, one of the servants,' she lied.

'Since when do servants wear stripy tights?' he frowned. He stood on the kitchen table and tried the slipper on Cillyderella's foot.

'Perfect fit,' he declared, 'this is the foot of my Princess!'

'No, you're making a terrible mistake. It can't be that wretched girl. You haven't tried it on Griselda yet...'

'I don't have to.' He dashed upstairs and kicked open the door of Cillyderella's room.

The Scary Godmother turned down the music.

'Oh, hello,' said Cillyderella, smiling.

The Prince's face lit up. 'It is you!' He rushed to gently pull her out of the floor.

'I'm a terrible mess,' she blushed.

'You're... wonderful! Will you come to the palace and be my Princess?' he asked her, bending down on one knee.

'I'd love to!' said Cillyderella happily.

'You'll pay for that damage!' Lady Muggly shouted bitterly after them as they all left in the royal carriage.

'You can send the bill to the palace,' the footman called back, grinning smugly.

Soon, Cillyderella and the Prince were married. The King and Queen were so proud - and relieved. The Scary Godmother was chief bridesmaid. But spoilsports Lady Muggly, Felicity and Griselda didn't come.

The Prince and Cillyderella lived happily ever after, though the Prince preferred to call his new wife, Princess Ella, as he didn't think she was one bit silly.

What do you think?

Also available in the Reluctant Reader Series from:

PUBLISHING

The Curse of the Full Moon *(Mystery)*
Stephanie Baudet   ISBN 978 1 904904 11 3

A Marrow Escape *(Adventure)*
Stephanie Baudet   ISBN 1 900818 82 5

The One That Got Away *(Humorous)*
Stephanie Baudet   ISBN 1 900818 87 6

The Haunted Windmill *(Mystery)*
Margaret Nash   ISBN 978 1 904904 22 9

Trevor's Trousers *(Humorous)*
David Webb   ISBN 978 1 904904 19

The Library Ghost *(Mystery)*
David Webb   ISBN 978 1 904374 66

Dinosaur Day   *(Adventure)*
David Webb   ISBN 978 1 904374 67 1

Friday the Thirtheenth *(Humorous)*
David Webb   ISBN 978 1 905637 37 9

The Curse of the Pharaoh's Tomb *(Adventure)*
David Webb   ISBN 978 1 905637 42 3

Laura's Game   *(Football)*
David Webb   ISBN 1 900818 61 2

Grandma's Teeth *(Humorous)*
David Webb   ISBN 978 1 905637 20 1

Snakes Legs and Cows Eggs *(Humorous)*
Adam Bushnell   ISBN 978 1 905637 21 8

Order online @ **www.eprint.co.uk**